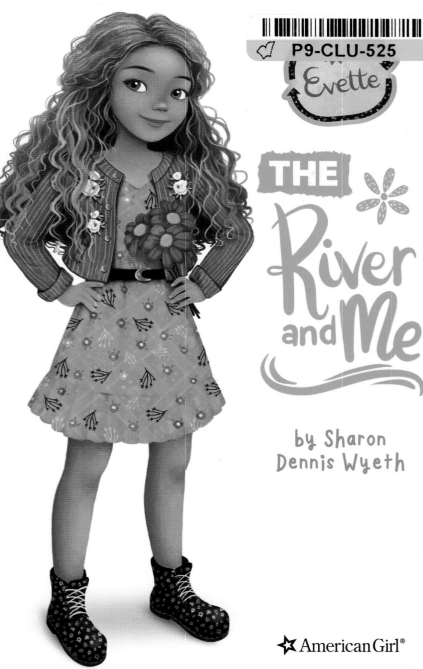

P9-CLU-525

Evette

THE

River and Me

by Sharon
Dennis Wyeth

★ American Girl®

FOR SHERI DENNIS ISAAC, 12-YEAR VETERAN OF THE DC METRO AND DR. SHELLEY GLOVER, TWO ESSENTIAL WORKERS IN MY FAMILY DURING THE 2020 CORONAVIRUS PANDEMIC
—SDW

ABOUT THE AUTHOR

Sharon Dennis Wyeth was born and raised in Washington, DC. She's written lots of books, but her first publishing experience was at Anacostia High School, where she was editor in chief of the yearbook. She also started the Southeast Teen Lounge, where she and her classmates got together to listen to music, eat hot dogs, and talk about news of the day. She loves hiking and owns a red canoe. She lives in New Jersey, but will always love DC's Anacostia River. Her many books include *Something Beautiful, The World of Daughter McGuire,* and *Always My Dad,* a Reading Rainbow book.

ABOUT THE ILLUSTRATOR

Olivia Duchess has loved drawing since she was a child growing up in London, where she still lives and works. Her earliest memories consist of drawing and illustrating comics and short stories. She also loves to swim and play video games, and she has a kitten called Mr. Nibbles.

ADVISERS FOR EVETTE'S STORY

Katrina Lashley is a program coordinator at Smithsonian's Anacostia Community Museum. Her Urban Waterways Project looks at cities and their watersheds, documenting community engagement, activism, and environmental advocacy. She also leads the Women's Environmental Leadership Initiative.

Yasmine Mabene is a student at Stanford University. A teen activist, she is the California State Director of March for Our Lives, a youth organization working to prevent gun violence, and the social media coordinator of Earth Uprising, an international youth-led organization that works to fight climate change through education.

M. Lucero Ortiz is a human rights attorney with a focus on family and immigration law. Prior to joining Kids in Need of Defense as the Deputy Director for KIND Mexico, she represented migrant families and unaccompanied children before the Departments of Homeland Security and Justice.

Deborah Rivas-Drake is a professor of psychology and education at the University of Michigan, where she studies how teens navigate issues of race, ethnicity, racism, and xenophobia. She wrote the award-winning book *Below the Surface: Talking with Teens about Race, Ethnicity, and Identity*.

Deanna Singh leads workshops on creating impactful social and personal change. She founded Flying Elephant, a consulting firm to help women and people of color become social entrepreneurs. She has written four children's books about racism, including *A Smart Girl's Guide: Race & Inclusion*.

Naomi Wadler is a 14-year-old activist concerned with racial justice. She focuses on optimism in the face of current events. She's interested in how journalism and media can influence others and make the world a better place. At age 11 she was the youngest speaker at the 2018 March for Our Lives rally in Washington, DC.

Hi! We're Evette, Makena, and Maritza. We want to live in a world where everyone is treated fairly and with respect. We believe that if we work together, we can build a future that works for all of us. Best of all, we don't need to wait until we grow up to make a difference— we can do it right now! Together, we have the power to create the kind of world we want: *a world by us.*

ABOUT ME,
Evette Peeters

Me, Evette!
Nickname: Evie

13 years old

I live in: **WASHINGTON, DC**

With:
MOM · · · a doctor
DAD · · · a builder
and
BUD · a pesky brother

♡ **I LIKE:**

UPCYCLING
re-use it!

NATURE

anything **VINTAGE**

EQUALITY

family **1ST**

swimming

I DISLIKE:

RACISM

Litterbugs

Pandemics

FARM & GARDEN SUPPLY

MEXICAN SUNFLOWER SEEDS

500mg

GRANDMA AND
GRANDPA PEETERS

GRAN E
(FOR EVON)

ME, MARITZA, AND
MAKENA: BFFS!

NURTURE
NATURE

ESSENTIAL

Chapter 1

In my family's front yard, beneath a spreading maple tree, there's a sign that reads, "Thank You Essential Workers!" When we made that sign last year, I painted a monarch butterfly above the words. Monarchs fly thousands of miles. Their strength and endurance remind me of the people who were on the front lines during the pandemic.

On the sign, my brother, Bud, drew an earthworm. "They're essential workers for the earth, because they make soil," Bud explained. He's ten. I don't like touching worms the way he does, but after a year of gardening with our grandmother Evon, I get why they're important.

When Mom and Dad saw what Bud and I had done, they put pictures on the sign, too. Mom drew a heart, because she's a pediatric cardiologist—a doctor who fixes children's hearts. Dad drew a nail, since he builds houses. Except Dad's nail looked like a pencil.

"It's a nail," Dad insisted. "I build houses, and you can't put up a house without nails."

"How about a sandcastle?" Bud piped up.

"Or an igloo?" I chimed in.

"Or a gingerbread house?" teased Mom.

Dad grinned. "You got me. Those would save money on nails, for sure!"

Things are getting back to normal now. Tomorrow is the first day of school, and I'll be starting seventh grade. Sixth grade—last year—was my first year in middle school, but it didn't feel like it, since most of the year was virtual learning. It was hard to make friends. How can you get to know people when all you have to go on are tiny pictures of their heads crowded together on a computer screen?

This year will be different. I can't wait to see my best friend, Ashlyn. We FaceTimed a lot during the pandemic, but it wasn't the same as hanging out in real life. Ashlyn has been in Maine with her dad all summer, so tomorrow's the day we'll finally be together again!

There are two other people I still haven't seen in person: Grandma and Grandpa Peeters. They live here in DC, same as my family, but when the pandemic hit, they stopped having visitors. Grandpa Peeters has health issues, so it was too dangerous for him to be exposed to other people's germs. Not seeing them all this time has been really hard. (Okay—I've seen them on video calls, but it's not the same. For one thing, they never adjusted their monitor the right way, so we often saw their kitchen ceiling instead of them.)

Last year Grandma Peeters sent me a silver heart-shaped necklace and a note in calligraphy:

> *My Sweet Evette,*
>
> *We may be apart,*
> *but we are always*
> *close in heart.*
>
> *All my love,*
> *Grandma*

Grandma Peeters taught me how to do calligraphy years ago, so all through the pandemic, we sent each other notes written with beautiful swirling letters. I always included sketches on my notes—butterflies and cherry blossoms and sunflowers—and Grandma says each one is a piece of art. She told me she has all of them displayed in the sunroom. I saved all the notes she sent me, too, and I've worn the heart necklace every day.

Luckily, we were still able to see Gran E. She's our mom's mother, and she was part of our pod from the beginning of the pandemic. While our parents went to work, Bud and I went to Gran E's house. Gran made sure we got our school-work done, and then she made sure we did something useful with our free time.

"No more screens," Gran E would announce when we logged off virtual school. The three of us played board games, baked bread, and did lots of crafts. Gran saves everything, so she always had plenty of craft supplies for us to use. Bud made a whole cardboard city for his Matchbox cars, and I helped him paint the buildings and roads. I made bird feeders out of milk cartons and hung them in the backyard. Bud and I even showed Gran how to make slime, but after one batch she said, "I think I'll stick with bread dough."

When spring arrived, Gran showed us how to plant seeds and grow flowers and vegetables. The one good thing about not going anywhere was seeing the gardens change. I never knew it could be fun to watch plants grow, but it actually was. Once when I saw a squirrel nibbling our baby sunflower plants, I flew outside with a bag of sunflower seeds and flung the seeds at the squirrel like confetti, shouting, "Eat this instead!"

My favorite thing to do at Gran E's is explore her

bedroom closet, which is full of old clothes. She doesn't wear them anymore, but she believes in saving anything that might still be put to good use. One day I found a blue and white dress with bell sleeves and a fluttery hem. It looked so pretty, but it was too big for me. "Can I wear this someday, Gran?" I asked, holding the dress up against me in front of the mirror.

"Why wait for someday?" Gran E said. "Let's make it fit you now." That's when Gran began teaching me how to sew.

I spent a long time putting my outfit together for the first day of school tomorrow. I decided on cropped jeans, a striped denim jacket that I embroidered myself, plus an awesome pair of platform shoes that Gran E wore when she was a teenager. I took a photo and sent it as a DM to Makena, this girl I follow online. She's right here in DC, just like me, and she always posts a cool OOTD—that means outfit of the day. With my photo, I wrote,

My first-day outfit. Check out the platforms! —Evette P.

When that was done, I plopped onto my bed and started to text Ashlyn. I got as far as, "Let's meet at—" when Mom knocked on my door and came in.

"Tomorrow morning, I get to drive you and Bud to school," she announced, sounding pleased. In the past year, Mom had worked such long hours at the hospital that Bud and I hadn't seen much of her.

I grinned. "That'll be cool, Mom."

She smoothed my quilt. "Do you have the school supplies you need for tomorrow?"

"They're in the backpack Grandma and Grandpa Peeters sent me," I told her. "When are we going to see them, anyway?" I asked.

"As a matter of fact, that brings me to my next bit of news," Mom said. "Grandpa had a checkup today, and his doctor said it's safe for us to visit."

"Yay!" I cheered. "When can we go?"

"This weekend," Mom answered. "They've invited us over."

"Great! I've missed them. And it's been so hot—I can't wait to swim in their pool."

She kissed me on the cheek and gave me a hug. "Good night, Evie. I love you."

"Mom, please, I'm thirteen! You don't need to kiss me good night."

She smiled. "I know—but I want to." I rolled my eyes, but I hugged and kissed her good night, too.

When Mom left, I finished texting Ashlyn.

Let's meet at the yellow bench by school door 👍

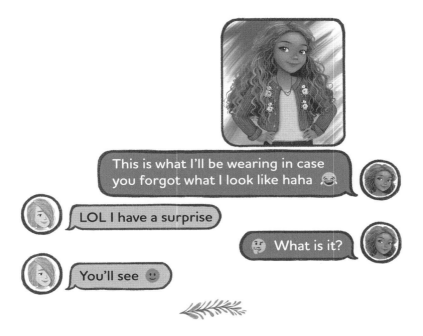

This is what I'll be wearing in case you forgot what I look like haha 😂

LOL I have a surprise

What is it? 🤔

You'll see 🙂

Sitting in Mom's car the next morning, looking out at the mash of kids gathering on the lawn of the middle school, I felt butterflies in my stomach. My elementary school was so much smaller.

"Will you be okay in those shoes?" Mom asked, glancing down at my feet.

"Mo-om, stop worrying about me! If Gran E could wear these back in her day, then so can I." I opened the car door. Mom's eyes looked kind of teary. "It's okay, Mom," I said, patting her hand. "It's not like I'm going off to college."

She laughed and hugged me. I grabbed my backpack and jumped out of the car. As I made my way through the crowd of kids toward the yellow bench, I recognized faces from virtual school and waved to old friends from elementary school. Suddenly I heard laughter and saw three kids standing by the yellow bench, a boy and two girls. One of the girls looked familiar. I realized it was Ashlyn—except her hair was pink!

"Hey, Ashlyn!" I called, hurrying over.

"Hey, Evette," she said.

I tried not to stare at her head. Now that I was close up, I saw that one side was long and the other was shaved. That must have been the surprise she mentioned. Good thing she had warned me; I was definitely surprised. Ashlyn's friends looked kind of freaky, too. The girl's hair was a flat black that looked fake, and she had on so much eyeliner that she looked like one of those ancient Egyptian mummy masks at the National Museum. And the boy's pants hung so far down, I could see his skull-and-crossbones boxers.

"Do you know Gia and Ziggy?" Ashlyn asked, pointing to her friends. "We were in the same homeroom last year."

"You know, virtual homeroom," said Ziggy.

"So boring," said Gia. "Except when Ziggy sends crazy selfies."

The three of them started laughing again. It was obviously an inside joke.

"I wish *we* were in the same homeroom," I told Ashlyn, trying not to look at her semi-shaved head.

"I know," said Ashlyn. "Mega-bummer. How do you like my hair? Gia cut it for me."

"It's, um, a big change," I stammered.

"I could do your hair, too," Gia offered.

"Uh, thanks, I'll think about it," I said, to be polite. I already knew I did *not* want a half-shaved head.

"I saw you get out of the car," said Ziggy. "Was that your mom who dropped you off?" I nodded, and he squinted at me as if trying to decide something. "So—are you Black or White?"

I bristled. I hadn't asked about Ziggy's race. How come he was asking about mine? Did I need to be one or the other? "My mother's side of our family is Black,

and my father's side is White," I explained. "So I'm both."

I turned and grabbed Ashlyn's arm. "Let's eat lunch together?" I asked, hoping she understood I meant just her, not her friends.

"Sure, Evie," she said, breaking free. "See you later."

The bell rang, and we all streamed toward the front doors of the school.

When lunch rolled around, I hurried to the cafeteria, eager to see Ashlyn, but when I finally got there, Ashlyn, Ziggy, and Gia were already finished eating.

"Sorry, Evie," said Ashlyn. "We were starving."

I shrugged to hide my disappointment and hurt feelings. It seemed like my friendship with Ashlyn might be over. She had made it clear that being friends with me wasn't essential.

SUNFLOWERS
Chapter 2

After school, Gran E's car was waiting outside. Bud was sitting next to her in the front seat.

"Hop in!" Gran E called cheerfully.

"Hi, Evie!" said Bud.

"Hi," I muttered, climbing into the back.

I turned on my phone and looked at Makena's Instagram. She had a cute post of her first-day-of-school outfit—a cropped black jacket and a pleated skirt, with gold butterflies clipped in her hair. I added a like to her page and a butterfly emoji. I looked at her photos but didn't see my platform shoes.

"All right back there?" Gran E asked, meeting my eyes in the rearview mirror. "How was school?"

It was too hard to explain what I was feeling about Ashlyn and her friends. "Not exactly what I expected," I finally said, pressing my nose to the window. The bridge was coming up. Pretty soon, we'd be crossing the Anacostia. I'd been crossing that river all my life on the way to Gran E's house. Every time I saw it, the river looked different. Sometimes the waves were rough, but today they were calm. The sunlight made the pale green water sparkle.

"Look at that awesome sailboat," Bud called out. "I'm gonna buy me one of those babies."

"No doubt you will someday," Gran E replied with a chuckle. "Today we have other plans."

"What are we doing?" I asked.

"We'll stop at my house and get some vegetables from the garden, and then take them to Riverfront Community Center," said Gran.

"It's finally open?" I asked.

Gran E nodded. "They opened last week."

"Why are we taking vegetables there?" asked Bud.

"For the food pantry," Gran E explained. "I hear they also have an art gallery."

"What if the food gets on the art?" said Bud.

"I'm sure they've thought of that," Gran E said dryly.

"Some families in the community need help getting enough food," I reminded Bud. "I'm glad we're donating some of the food we grew."

Gran E parked in front of her cozy redbrick house, and we followed her through the front door.

"Bud, grab the pitchfork and go dig up some potatoes," said Gran, charging through the living room toward the kitchen.

My phone dinged with a notification. I checked it—and

saw that Makena had posted my photo and tagged me! She'd written, *Love the platforms, Evette P. Show me more!*

Makena liked my shoes! I held up the phone so Gran E could see. "Your shoes are famous!"

Gran E stopped and peered at the screen. "Well, how about that. Who posted that picture?"

"A girl named Makena," I told her. "I follow her fashion posts. Hey, can I grab that butterfly scarf from your closet? I wanted to send a photo to Makena. She likes butterflies."

"Be quick about it," Gran E said.

"Earth to Evie! Earth to Gran!" Bud shouted through the window. He was already in the backyard. "I'm doing all the work here!"

"Coming, Bud!" Gran E called back.

"I'll be there in a minute," I promised.

As the back door slammed, I ran upstairs to Gran E's bedroom. On the wall there was a handsome picture of Grandpa Paul, who died before I was born. I opened Gran's closet. On the top shelf was a basket of yarn along with some folded scarves, but the one with butterflies wasn't there. I kept looking. Tucked in the corner behind a pile of purses, I saw something wrapped in tissue paper. I picked it up and opened the tissue paper. It was a swim-suit! A beautiful bright yellow one-piece, covered with sunflowers—my favorite flower. And it looked like my size! Forgetting my search for the butterfly scarf, I hurried down to the backyard with the swimsuit.

"Look at all this stuff!" Bud cried when he saw me. He pointed to a cardboard box half filled with potatoes, tomatoes, and carrots. On top was a giant green squash.

"That's quite a haul," I agreed. "How do you like this swimsuit I found?"

Bud shrugged. "It's okay, I guess."

"Where'd you find that thing?" asked Gran E, casting a cool eye toward the swimsuit. "I can't believe I kept it."

"It was in the back of your closet," I said. "It's very cute."

Gran's mouth turned down. "Cute all right," she agreed. "Maybe that was part of the trouble."

"What trouble?" I asked. "It has my favorite flower! It looks like it's hardly been worn."

"I wore it just once," said Gran, "and that was enough. It was the one and only time I went to the public pool. In my sunflower swimsuit, I thought I was in style. But it didn't make a bit of difference to those people at the pool.

"As soon as I stepped to the edge of the pool, some White girls began to mock me. The thought that a little Black girl would dare to come to their pool dressed in a stylish suit and think that she'd actually be able to swim . . ." Gran E shook her head.

I swallowed. "Then what happened?"

"I never even got into the water," said Gran E. "Those White kids made it clear I wasn't welcome. I ran home. And I never wore my new sunflower swimsuit again."

A pain rose in my chest. "I won't wear the swimsuit if it makes you sad," I told her.

"Nonsense," said Gran. "Put it to good use. Anyway, after that incident at the public pool, I found a much better place to swim."

"Where was it?" Bud asked curiously.

"A beautiful swimming hole on the river," Gran said, smiling. "After that, I never went back to that pool."

"You should come to Grandma and Grandpa Peeters's pool," said Bud as he bit into a carrot.

"Hey, we're going to their house this weekend," I said. "You should come with us!"

Gran E frowned. "I wouldn't go swimming in their pool if you paid me." She said the words as if there was something awful-tasting in her mouth.

"What do you mean?" I asked, taken aback.

"It's too far for me to go traipsing up to their neck of the woods," she grumbled, looking flustered. "I don't have time for those people."

"Are you—are you upset with Grandma and Grandpa Peeters?" I asked uncertainly.

"Bud, we could use some turnips in this box," Gran said briskly.

"Yes, ma'am," said Bud, grabbing the trowel.

"And Evette, you're welcome to keep that swimsuit. Now, let's get a move on."

From her tone, it was clear that Gran E was done talking about my other grandparents. I looked at the sunflower swimsuit I was holding. The bright print gave me an idea. "Maybe we could take some flowers to the community center," I suggested.

"People can't eat flowers," said Bud.

"We can take a bouquet as a gift," I said. "To say congratulations to Riverfront for opening."

"That's very thoughtful," Gran agreed.

I picked up the gardening shears and walked to the flower bed. That spring we'd planted daisies and sunflowers. The sunflowers had come up bright orange with yellow centers.

"I can't believe how orange these sunflowers are," I exclaimed, admiring their fiery color. "Most sunflowers are yellow."

"Different kind of seeds," Gran reminded me. "These are Mexican sunflowers. Remember? We read that on the seed package."

As I clipped flowers for the bouquet, I glanced over at Gran E, digging turnips with Bud. When she was young, White girls had chased her out of a pool just because of her skin color. At school that morning, Ziggy had asked about my race, as if that would tell him who I was—but in reality, it wouldn't tell him anything about what kind of a person, or friend, I might be. Why did people think skin color defines who we are? It seemed so simple: humans come in different colors, just like flowers.

MAKENA AND MARITZA

Chapter 3

On our way to Riverfront Community Center, Gran E told Bud and me about her swimming place on the river.

"Was it as wide and deep as the Anacostia River?" Bud asked.

Gran laughed. "My swimming hole certainly wasn't as big as the Anacostia. It was a tributary—a stream that feeds into the Anacostia."

"Who lives around there?" asked Bud.

"Well, the original people who lived there long ago were the Anacostan people," Gran replied. "Now we call them Native Americans. But when I was growing up, the neighborhood was Black, just like it is today."

"When was the last time you were there?" I asked.

"Not since I was a kid," said Gran E. "Maybe the three of us could go and find it."

Bud and I looked at each other. "Road trip!" we said at the exact same time.

Riverfront Community Center is a big, modern building that overlooks the Anacostia River. We parked and crossed a broad lawn to the main doors. In the front lobby was a huge mural of Anacostia Park. It showed people of all ages and colors running, biking, dancing, and playing music, with the river flowing in the background. I wanted to stop and look at it, but Gran E hustled us along. Inside, Gran and Bud followed the sign that pointed to the food pantry while I stopped at the reception desk.

"These are for the community center," I told the receptionist, presenting the flowers. "My grandmother and I grew them ourselves."

"How lovely!" she said.

"Is there somewhere I should put them? I guess I should have brought a vase."

"Check the lounge at the end of the corridor," she directed. "I bet there's a vase on one of the shelves, and you can get water there, too."

The room at the end of the corridor had a large table and lockers full of craft supplies. One whole wall was a giant window of clear and colored glass, looking out onto the river. The late afternoon sun was low in the sky, giving the water a golden glow and making pools of color on the walls and floor.

I found a pretty blue vase and filled it. As I was

arranging the orange sunflowers in the vase, a girl in a soccer uniform came in.

"I was told I'd find water here," she said, holding up her water bottle.

I pointed to the water station on the wall. "Is there a soccer game today?" I asked.

"Team practice," she said, filling her bottle. "Nice sunflowers," she added, nodding at my arrangement. "I've never seen them that color before."

"They're from Mexico," I explained.

The girl smiled. "Hey, my grandparents are from Mexico, too!"

"Really? I'd love to go to Mexico someday," I told her. "Have you been there?" The girl nodded. "What's it like?" I asked.

She plopped down onto the couch. "Warm—and there's lots of great food," she said. "My mom's from Bolivia. Both sides of my family love visiting us here in DC. Next year we're hosting a big family reunion!"

"That sounds like fun," I said with envy. The two sides of my family live in the same city, but they never got together.

"I'm Evette," I told her. "What's your name?"

"Maritza." She smiled. "My friends call me Itza."

I smiled back. Hearing Maritza describe her family made me think, *Maybe my family could have a reunion, too.*

On our way back to the lobby, Maritza and I stopped at the art exhibit. Vivid colors of yarn and string were knitted into dazzling patterns and textures. I wanted to reach out and touch them.

"Wow," said someone behind me.

"I know, right?" I said, turning around.

A girl with black hair in long twists was gazing at my shoes. She looked up at me and smiled brightly. "I recognize those shoes! Are you Evette P?" It was Makena!

"Makena, whoa, I can't believe it's really . . . you, in real life," I stammered. "Am I saying your name right? Ma*kay*na?"

"That's it." She pointed at my shoes. "So where'd you get those?"

I grinned. "From my grandma's closet!"

"Great find! Are they comfortable?" she asked.

I nodded. "Surprisingly, yes."

She smiled. "Do you live around here?"

"My grandma does," I told her. "Do you?"

"Born and bred in Anacostia," she replied proudly. "I help out at the food pantry."

"Sweet! This is my first time coming here. My brother and grandmother are donating veggies at the food pantry. And this is Maritza," I said, gesturing at my new friend.

"Hey," Makena said, nodding at Maritza, who smiled back. "So, what do you guys think of this art?" Makena asked.

"I like it!" said Maritza. "Bolivia is famous for colorful weaving. My mother and grandmother will have to see this—they'd like it, too."

"I'm learning how to knit, but I'm not that good at it yet," I told them. "Both of my grandmothers are great knitters, though."

"My grandma knits, too," said Makena. "She's offered to teach me to sew, but I haven't tried it yet." Makena grinned. "I'm more of a stylist than a seamstress."

"My grandma taught me how to sew," I said. "She showed me how to take something that doesn't fit right, or that I don't wear anymore, and turn it into something that I like better," I told them. "Like turn a dress into a top, or old pants into a bag. You know—upcycling."

"You'll have to show me some of your projects, and I'll post them." Makena whipped out her phone and we all exchanged numbers.

"Maybe we could go thrift shopping sometime," I suggested.

"I'm in!" said Maritza. "That sounds fun."

Makena grinned. "Totally! Let's do it."

As I headed back to the car with Gran and Bud, my heart felt light. I had made two new friends, Makena and Maritza. I tried to put my disappointment about Ashlyn behind me.

NONE OF MY BUSINESS

Chapter 4

Dad was late picking us up from Gran E's house because his truck got a flat tire.

"Can you believe it?" he said at dinner. "I must have driven over one of my own nails at the building site!"

"Can the tire be repaired?" Mom asked.

"I'm not sure. I dropped it off at Stan's Garage, and he'll let me know tomorrow morning," said Dad. "My tires are getting old, but Stan said he'd take a look."

"How was your first day at school?" Mom asked, pouring the milk.

"Mine was great," said Bud. "We played basketball."

"How about you?" Dad asked, offering me the salad.

"It was so-so." I grabbed a cherry tomato and popped it into my mouth. "But Gran E took us to that new community center, Riverfront. It's got all this beautiful art. And I met some girls there."

"Gran's going to take us to her special beach on the river," Bud piped up.

Mom squinted. "Special beach? Where's that?"

"It's where Gran used to swim when she was a girl,"

I explained. "She says it's a really pretty spot."

"Lucky you!" said Mom.

Later, shortly before bed, Mom came into my room. I was in my beanbag chair, reading a chapter for social studies.

"Hey there," she said, perching on the side of the bed. "Is everything okay at school?" Clearly her mom radar was sensing something.

I shrugged.

"Was it nice to be with Ashlyn again?" Mom asked.

"Ashlyn's different and has different friends now," I said flatly. Mom looked surprised. "She

said she would eat lunch with me—but she ate with them instead." I closed my book. "Whatever, it's fine."

Mom nodded. "Well, people do change, but you and Ashlyn have been friends for so long. Don't give up on her."

"I'd rather just make new friends," I said, telling her about Makena and Maritza.

"It's nice to make new friends," said Mom, "but old friends can't be replaced. You have a shared past."

"Ashlyn made it pretty clear she would rather be with her other friends. They were in homeroom together last year, and now they're together again," I explained.

"Well, don't hold it against her," Mom said gently. "And try to be open-minded about her friends."

"They were dressed all weird," I muttered. "Ashlyn's hair was half pink, half shaved. Her new friend Gia did it for her. Ashlyn's friends—well, they're just not my type."

Mom raised her eyebrows. "You can't tell what people are really like until you get to know them. You know the saying, don't judge a book by its cover? If Ashlyn likes them, you might like them, too."

Instead of answering, I got up to put on my pajamas. I had made them myself from an old seersucker pantsuit of Mom's that she didn't wear anymore. I wouldn't be caught dead wearing it as a pantsuit, but the cotton fabric was light and cool and comfy, so Gran E helped me tighten the elastic waist, shorten the pants, and move the buttons on the top to make it smaller, and it made perfect pj's. I put them on and hung my heart necklace on my jewelry tree. Next to it was a locket that had an umoja symbol on it. *Umoja* means "unity" in the Swahili language. Gran E had given me the locket for Kwanzaa last year, along with a card that said, "Promise always to seek umoja: unity in the family, community, nation, and race."

As I fingered the locket, I asked Mom, "What's the deal with Gran E and Grandma Peeters? Do they not like each other?"

Mom blinked. "We were discussing you and your friends. Not your grandmothers."

"But today when Bud and I invited Gran E to go swimming at Grandma and Grandpa Peeters's house with us this weekend, Gran said that she wouldn't swim in their pool if we paid her."

Mom rolled her eyes. "Yeah, that sounds like my mother. She can be stubborn."

"Why did she say that?" I pressed.

Mom paused. Finally she said quietly, "Something happened between them, but it was long ago and best forgotten."

"I knew it!" Mom wasn't the only one with radar. Setting

down the unity necklace, I turned and looked at her. "Your family and Dad's never spend holidays together. Other families have reunions, and both sides come even when they live in different countries. Ours live in the same city, and they never see each other, or see us at the same time."

"Settle down, Evie," said Mom. "You're making a big deal out of something that happened before you were born."

"What was it?" I asked.

"Nothing you can do anything about. Dredging it up will be hurtful for everyone," she said. "It's ancient history. Besides, it's none of your business."

I got into bed. Mom hugged and kissed me good night. I didn't hug her back like I usually do. When she closed the door to my room, I rolled over and faced the wall. For some reason, I could feel tears trying to squeeze their way out of my eyes. Two of the people I loved most in the world didn't like each other! But why? Mom had said it wasn't my business, but they were my family, so it affected me. Didn't that make it my business? Didn't I have a right to know?

Suddenly Ziggy's question popped into my head. *Are you Black or White?*

Gran E was Black, like Mom. Grandma and Grandpa Peeters were White, like Dad. Did that have something to do with it?

THINGS IN THE PAST

Chapter 5

The next morning I woke up early. I found Dad in the kitchen. He usually left the house before everyone else, but today he was going in later so he could pick up his tire at the garage.

"Want a ride to school?" Dad offered. "We can stop at the bakery for muffins."

That was all I needed to hear. I grabbed my backpack and we climbed into his truck and set off.

At our favorite bakery, I picked out a blueberry muffin and milk, and Dad got two apple cinnamon muffins and coffee. "Next stop, Stan's Garage," he announced, as we got back into his truck. The morning sunlight slanting through the windows had already warmed my seat. A feeling of happiness warmed me, too. It wasn't just the yummy muffins. It felt special to be in the truck with Dad. And, I realized, it was the perfect opportunity to ask him about the thing that had been bothering me from the minute I woke up: my grandmothers. Maybe *he* would be willing to tell me about it, whatever it was. But just as I was pondering how to bring it up, Dad brought it up himself.

"Your mother told me about your talk last night," he said, keeping his eye on the traffic.

I swallowed a bite of my muffin. "Yes, I found out that my grandmothers don't like each other, but Mom won't tell me why. What happened between them?"

"Best leave well enough alone," Dad advised, avoiding the question. "Both of your grandmothers love you, and that's what matters."

"I know, and I love them, too. That's why I want to know what happened," I pressed.

"Suppose your grandmothers don't *want* you to know?" Dad said. "People have a right to privacy. Don't stir things up, Evie. Your mother and I decided long ago that it was best to leave things alone."

"What *things*?" I persisted.

"Things in the past. Things that don't matter anymore."

"They matter to me, if they're standing in the way of us being together as a family," I pointed out.

"No family is perfect," Dad said, pulling off the road into a small parking lot. A sign on the building said STAN'S GARAGE. Dad parked and turned to me. "Your mother and I tried to mend the rift, but we couldn't. Sometimes it's best to let bygones be bygones. Now, let's see if Stan was able to fix my flat."

Dad got out and went into the shop. Sitting in the truck,

I stared at the bakery bag in my lap. So there was a rift in our family—a rift that Dad and Mom couldn't mend. Suddenly the muffin felt dry in my mouth, and I wasn't hungry anymore.

The shop door opened, and a man came out with Dad. I could hear the man saying, "I'll have those new tires here by this afternoon, if you can stop by then. It won't take long to swap them out." They shook hands, and then walked over to the truck. The man peeked in the window and smiled at me.

"This is my daughter, Evette," said Dad as he got in and started up the truck. "Thanks again, Stan. See you this afternoon."

"I appreciate the work," said Stan, waving. "The pandemic was tough on business."

"What about your tire?" I asked, as we rolled out of the parking lot.

"It was shot," Dad said. "My tires are old, and the treads

are worn. Stan's going to put on a new set this afternoon."

"Why was the pandemic tough on Stan's business?" I asked.

"Well, since people stayed home and didn't drive as much, they didn't need as many car repairs, so Stan didn't get as much business. A lot of small businesses ran out of money and had to close," Dad said. "I'm glad Stan managed to stay open. He's a good mechanic."

We had arrived at my school. I unbuckled my seat belt and shouldered my backpack. "Thanks for the ride, Dad." I hopped out of the truck.

"Have a great day, honey. See you tonight," he called as he pulled away from the curb.

STAN'S GARAGE

That day at school, and the next, I avoided Ashlyn. It was easy to do, since we didn't have any classes together. I passed her once in the hall, but I kept my eyes straight ahead and pretended I didn't see her.

Still, I couldn't help wondering, *Is this how a rift gets started?* Something goes wrong between people, and they avoid each other, and before you know it, there's a rift between them. Was that how it happened with my grandmothers?

And the most important question of all: Could a rift between people ever be repaired?

A SIGHT TO BEHOLD

Chapter 6

On Thursday, Gran E picked us up after school again. As I neared the car, Bud called out the window, "Hurry up! Gran's taking us to her special beach!"

I opened the door, tossed my backpack onto the back seat, and climbed in.

"Gran made a picnic cake," Bud reported, pointing to a picnic basket on the floor next to me.

"Red velvet?" I asked hopefully.

"What else?" Gran replied.

My mouth was watering already. Gran made the best red velvet cake, but she only made it for picnics, so it was a real treat.

As we drove over the bridge to Anacostia, I gazed out the window. The big river churned with restless waves.

"Gran, how did you find your special swimming hole?" asked Bud.

"My big brother Robert showed it to me," said Gran. "It was the very same day those girls chased me away from the public pool. I ran home, and Robert found me crying on the front porch.

"He told me not to worry about those mean kids. Then he showed me the swimming spot. It was only a few miles from our house—we could walk there ourselves.

"At the end of a quiet dead-end street, we turned down a path, and before I knew it, we were standing in front of a river. I remember seeing lots of birds, especially a tall cormorant standing on a rock out in the water."

Gran E turned down a dead-end street, parked the car, and we all got out. Bud and I followed as Gran led us down a gravel path and into the woods. I heard birds singing and smelled the scent of pine. Some of the trees were old and huge. The ground was covered with ferns and brambles.

"Oh, this old place brings back such happy memories," said Gran. "It's a sight to behold."

"I wish we had our swimsuits with us," said Bud.

"We'll take off our shoes and go wading," said Gran.

Bud and I grinned at each other. Gran E's excitement was catching. Through the tree branches, we caught flashes of silvery water. But as we stepped out of the trees, the scene changed. Plastic bags, bottles, and metal cans littered the shoreline and floated on the water. Chunks of Styrofoam were caught in a fallen tree at the water's edge. I spotted a waterlogged armchair and half-sunk lawn mower. And tires everywhere, stuck in the mud, bobbing in the water, and strewn along the bank.

It was a sight to behold, all right—but not the one we were expecting.

Bud looked around, his mouth open. "You used to swim *here*?"

Gran's shoulders drooped. "This isn't the way it looked back then," she said in a quavering voice. "Our swimming hole was clean and beautiful. But now—" She turned away. "I can't even look at it. Let's go," she said sharply, and began walking back up the path.

"Wait for us, Gran," called Bud, running after her.

A SIGHT TO BEHOLD

I lingered, taking a last look around. I noticed an old picnic table under a tree, but who would want to have a picnic here? Gran E had been so excited to see her river again—we all had—and now her memory was ruined.

My heart ached for her—and for the river, too. There were no cormorants to be seen here. Were there even fish or frogs living in all this garbage? From my earth science class in fifth grade, I knew that the Anacostia River was polluted and the city was trying to clean it up. I'd always thought the big river looked beautiful and mysterious, but I'd never looked closely at it or wondered what was beneath the water's surface. It had been easy to forget about pollution. But now, seeing this place and knowing what it had meant to my grandmother made the pollution feel real. *People* had done this, dumped stuff in the river. Ruined a beautiful place. Damaged nature. Didn't they even care? I wanted to fix it, but the problem was too big.

CANNONBALL
Chapter 7

We arrived at Grandma and Grandpa Peeters's house
Saturday morning. Their large yellow house with the white
columns on the porch was even prettier than I remembered.
Our grandparents threw their arms around us. I'd missed
them so much!

"Look how tall and lanky you are," Grandpa told Bud.

Grandma stroked my cheek. "You're so grown up, dear!"

"It's been a whole year since you've seen me, Grandma,"
I said.

She touched my heart necklace. "Always—" she began.

"—close in heart," we finished together.

Bud nudged me. "Earth to Evette. I hear a pool calling."

Grandma laughed. "It's been waiting for you!"

We went around to the backyard. Chips and lemonade
were set out on the patio table, but the first thing Bud and
I did was jump into the pool. While Grandpa chatted with
Mom and Dad on the patio and Bud practiced his cannonball, Grandma and I swam laps.

"What a cute suit," Grandma said. "I adore sunflowers."

"Thanks!" I said. "They're my favorite flowers, too."

Then I added, "Gran E gave it to me."

Grandma's eyes darted. "How is Evon?"

"She's fine. Well, except we found out that the place on the river where she used to swim is all polluted."

"That's terrible," said Grandma. "I'm sorry to hear that."

I floated on my back, looking up at the clouds, trying to decide how much to say.

We were having such a nice time, I hated to spoil it. Still, I wanted to know the truth about my grandmothers, and this was my chance.

"I know that something happened between you and Gran E a long time ago," I said, turning to face her. "What was it?"

Grandma looked startled. "Did Evon say something?"

"Sort of," I said, switching to sidestroke. I couldn't think of a nice way to put it, so I just told it the way it happened. "I invited her to come swimming with us today—and she said that she wouldn't swim here if somebody paid her."

Grandma caught her breath. There was a long silence, broken only by Bud shouting, "Cannonball!" followed by a huge splash.

When we reached the shallow end of the pool, Grandma stood, holding on to the edge, and began speaking in a low voice. "Evette, when your mother and father decided to get married, your grandpa and I were pleased. We knew your mother was a kind and accomplished young woman. But when your father told us that the wedding reception was to be at Evon's house, we—well, we wanted to have it here instead. Our house is bigger, and we imagined having guests around the pool and cutting the wedding cake on the patio."

"But Mom and Dad *did* have their reception here," I said. "I've seen the pictures in their album."

"Yes, and it was lovely," Grandma said. "But Evon wasn't happy about it. She left before Nia and Jason cut the wedding cake, and she's never come back since."

Grandma took a deep breath. "That day when your parents came over to tell us their wedding plans, I said that Evon's house was in a bad neighborhood, so we couldn't have the reception there."

"After the wedding, your mother let it go," said Grandma. "But your Gran E didn't."

I bit my lip. Gran E's neighborhood wasn't dangerous! It was full of her friends and neighbors. I had been going there all my life. Gran E's neighbors were my friends, too.

At first I felt shocked that Grandma Peeters would think this way. Then my heart began to ache. Because of what she had thought and said back then, a rift had opened between the two sides of our family, separating them. *This* was why we never had holidays with the whole family. *This* was why Gran E always seemed to be busy on our birthdays, and why, on Thanksgiving, we always had dinner at Gran E's house and dessert with Grandma and Grandpa Peeters. It had been this way my whole life, so I had taken it for granted and never questioned it. It was just how things were. But now, it suddenly felt raw and painful and made me feel very sad.

Without speaking, I climbed out of the pool and wrapped myself in a towel. Grandma got out, too, and put on her terry cloth robe. "Are you okay, honey?" she asked.

I took a deep breath. I loved Grandma, and I knew that she was a good person, but what she had said was wrong. "Just because Gran E lives in a Black neighborhood doesn't mean that it's filled with criminals," I told her. "That's—that's a racist thing to think. You probably weren't being racist on purpose, but what you said—and what you thought—that's racism." Grandma was silent. Finally I asked, "Have you ever even been to her neighborhood?"

Grandma Peeters shook her head. "I realize that I was wrong. I should never have said it. I wish I could take it back, but I can't."

"Did you ever apologize to Gran E?" I asked, curious.

"No. I was afraid to stir things up again," said Grandma. "We did invite Evon over to the house a number of times after that, hoping to smooth things over, but she always had an excuse not to come."

"Inviting someone to your house isn't the same as apologizing," I told her.

"That's true," Grandma agreed. "But how can I apologize if Evon refuses to speak with me?"

I reached out and touched her arm. She was trembling. Was she just chilled from the pool, or was this conversation as difficult for her as it was for me?

"I'm not proud of what I said back then," Grandma said quietly. "I love you and Bud and your mother. And I know Evon is wonderful to you all."

"We're all one family," I reminded her. "Can't you apologize now?"

"I think it's too late for that," said Grandma Peeters. "I should have said something long ago, but I kept thinking it would blow over. Now, fifteen years later, I wouldn't even know what to say. And I don't know that Evon would listen."

I wouldn't go swimming in their pool if you paid me. That's how Gran E felt. I knew it wasn't easy to change her mind. Maybe Grandma Peeters was right, and it was too late. Shivering in my towel, I left the pool to go get dressed.

IT'S PERSONAL
Chapter 8

The next day was Sunday, and I had arranged to meet Maritza and Makena at Riverfront. I was excited to see them again. Maritza and I met in the lounge and immediately started chatting. Soon Makena came in. We smiled and waved her over. But Makena didn't smile back.

"Is something wrong?" I asked, motioning for her to join us on the couch.

Makena plopped down beside us. "I was at the park yesterday with a boy from my neighborhood," she began. "We saw this little girl who was all alone. She looked about three. We were helping her find her mom, when this White woman started yelling at us." Makena paused. "The little girl was crying because she was lost, and the woman accused us of hurting her. Because the little girl was White and we're Black, the woman couldn't believe that we were trying to help." As Makena spoke, her face was a mix of anger and sadness. I put my hand on her arm.

"Did you find the girl's mom?" Maritza asked.

Makena nodded. "The girl's mom was grateful for our help. But the other White woman, the one who was yelling at us—when I tried to tell her the little girl was lost, she totally ignored me. She treated me like I wasn't even there." Makena swallowed. "And she treated my friend like he was dangerous, just because he's a Black boy."

I thought of Bud. He had brown skin, darker than mine. The idea of someone accusing my brother that way horrified me—but I could picture it all too easily, especially in a few years when he became a teenager.

"That could happen to my brother," I said softly. "He wouldn't hurt a worm, let alone a kid. But just because he's Black, some people might think—" I didn't finish the thought. I remembered the conversation yesterday at the pool with Grandma Peeters. This was the same thing: White people making assumptions about people of color, without any facts.

"It's discrimination," said Makena.

"It can happen in families, too," I said quietly.

Makena turned to me. "What do you mean?" she asked.

I hesitated for a moment. Mom had said that what went on between my two grandmothers wasn't my business. But I needed to talk about it with someone my own age—someone who would understand.

"My mom's side of our family is Black, and my dad's side is White. Yesterday, I found out that my White grandma said some horrible things to my other grandma years ago.

Grandma Peeters made assumptions about Gran E, just because she's Black."

The room was quiet. "That's racism," said Makena.

"In your own family," Maritza whispered.

I nodded, and before I knew what was happening, they were hugging me. "Thanks, guys," I said, hugging them back. "I wish I could do something to change things between my grandparents."

"Can you get them to talk about it?" Makena asked.

"I want to," I said, "but they completely avoid each other. It's been going on for years. That's the problem."

"That's really sad," said Maritza.

I nodded again. "It's all I've ever known, so I didn't realize before that anything was wrong."

I got up and went to the water fountain for a drink. Next to it was a flyer with a map of the Anacostia River. The flyer said, "Restore the river! To help, call Kasey." I pulled out my phone and called the number on the flyer.

"Hi, this is Kasey. Can I help you?" It sounded like an older teen or young man.

"My name is Evette Peeters," I said. "I want to restore a spot on the Anacostia River. It's a tributary," I explained.

"Great! Do you know the location of the tributary?" he asked.

I looked at the map on his flyer and read off the name

of the dead-end street where Gran E had parked the day we went to her swimming spot.

"I know exactly where that access point is," said Kasey. "If you can hustle up some volunteers, I can arrange a cleanup day. You'll need at least two adults."

"I can bring plenty of volunteers," I told him. "How soon can we do it?"

"How about next Saturday?" he asked. "Get your group organized, and I'll have equipment and a crew of volunteers from that neighborhood. We'll meet at the river at nine a.m."

"Great!" I said. "I'll get busy rounding people up."

"You sound very dedicated," Kasey said with a chuckle.

"I am," I said. "It's personal!"

When I got off the phone, Makena and Maritza crowded around me. "What was that about?" asked Maritza.

"I'm doing a river cleanup!" I told them.

"Wow," said Makena. "Where'd this come from?"

The three of us sat down again on the red couch, and I told them about Gran E's swimming spot. "She was crushed when she saw how polluted it is. Cleaning it up will take a lot of work."

"Count me in. I have soccer practice, but I'll talk to my coach," Maritza said staunchly.

"I'll come help, too," Makena promised.

"We'll have to wear old clothes," I warned her. "Wear

something you don't mind getting wet and muddy!"

Makena laughed. "I'm not afraid to get a little dirty. Especially for a good cause."

"It's funny," said Maritza. "A few minutes ago, we were all so serious. Now we're excited to do this."

"You're right," I agreed. "I can't wait to see Gran E's face when her swimming spot is cleaned up!"

"Will you invite your other grandmother, too?" asked Maritza.

The wheels in my head began turning. "If I do, they'll finally be in the same place at the same time—"

"—and they'll have to talk," Makena chimed in, reading my mind.

"Yes!" I said. "You know, I think this could work!"

When I got home, I told Mom and Dad about my plans for the river. "Can you all come?" I asked.

"I have hospital rounds this Saturday," said Mom. "But I'm impressed you're taking this on!"

"Bud and I will be there," said Dad. "Do you have enough volunteer labor?"

"I've got it, Dad," I assured him. "That's one thing social media is good for."

Next, I announced the river cleanup on my social media accounts. Then came the tricky part.

First, I put in a call to Grandma and Grandpa Peeters and told them what I was planning. I'd mentioned Gran E's swimming spot to Grandma when Bud and I had visited the day before. "And this Saturday, we're going to clean up all the trash, so it will be beautiful again, just like Gran E remembers it from when she was a girl."

"Sounds like a big project," said Grandpa. "I'll be glad to lend a hand."

"What a lovely idea," said Grandma. "I'm sure Evon will be touched by what you're doing. She'll be there, I presume?" she added, sounding a little nervous.

"Yes, I'm inviting her," I replied. "Maybe you two could talk." Grandma Peeters was quiet. "Please, Grandma?"

"As you know, Evette, I'm willing," she said, "but I can't make her speak to me."

"I know, Grandma. Thank you. See you there!" I ended the call, feeling lighter inside. There was just one last step.

I dialed my other grandmother. "Hi Gran E, it's Evette."

"Hi, sweetheart," she said.

"Guess what? I've organized a river cleanup on Saturday at your old swimming hole!"

"What do you mean?" she asked. I explained about Kasey and told her the plan.

"Evette, you never fail to amaze me," said Gran E. "When you decide to do something, you just do it."

"I learned that from you," I laughed. "Will you come?"

"Wild horses couldn't keep me away," she said. "How many folks will be helping us?"

"As many as I can get," I answered. "My friends, Kasey and other volunteers who live near the river, and our family. Our whole, entire family!"

Gran E was silent for a minute, just like Grandma Peeters had been.

"The whole, entire family, eh?" she said.

"It's a big project," I said. "We need everyone to pitch in."

"It's certainly good of you to take on such a worthy cause. Good night, Evette."

"Bye, Gran E! See you Saturday."

There—I'd invited both my grandmothers. The rest was up to them.

That night I made some flyers, and in school on Monday morning, I got permission to hang them up.

As I was taping my flyers to the wall outside the lunchroom, I saw Ashlyn reading one of them. I'd been avoiding her since school started, but now I realized I had been judging her, making assumptions about her that might not be fair— or accurate. And now I knew: the longer I waited to start talking to her again, the harder it would be.

Come to a
RIVER CLEANUP
This Saturday!

For info contact Evette Peeters.

Bring your lunch!

"Hey," I said, walking over to her.

"Hi Evie," she said. "I saw the same flyer in the library. You're doing a river cleanup?"

I nodded. "It's going to be fun. Want to come?"

"Sure," she said. "Anything I should bring?"

"Yeah—work gloves." We smiled at each other. Her pink hair had begun to look kind of cool. "Hey, we're still friends, right?" I ventured.

Ashlyn looked surprised. "Of course we are," she said. "Can Gia and Ziggy come to the river thing, too?"

I didn't blink. "The more the merrier."

"Cool," said Ashlyn. "We'll be there."

"Great," I said. Watching her rush off, I swallowed. I was getting used to the fact that I wasn't her only BFF, but I still hadn't forgotten the days when it had been just her and me. And I still didn't get Ziggy and Gia. But help was help, and the river needed all the help it could get.

CLEAN WATER ACTION
Chapter 9

The day of the river cleanup, I woke bright and early. Mom had already left for her hospital rounds, so after breakfast Dad drove Bud and me to the river. There were already quite a few cars parked at the dead end. Grandma and Grandpa Peeters met us there. I didn't see Gran E yet, but people were still arriving. Everyone was buzzing with excitement. I waved at Ashlyn, Ziggy, and Gia, who was wearing a "Save the Earth" T-shirt. I'd never figured Gia would care about the environment. So much for my assumptions!

More cars pulled in, and Maritza and Makena got out. I hurried over to greet them. As we chatted, a young man pulled up in an electric car. He got out and came over to our group, handing each of us a garbage bag. He looked about twenty.

"Hi, I'm Kasey," he said. "Who's the girl who called last Sunday?"

"Me! I'm Evette Peeters," I said shyly.

"Well, you sure delivered on volunteers. Thank you all for coming out," said Kasey. "Okay, let's go get that garbage out of the river!"

He led the whole troop of us down the gravel path. People began spreading out, picking up trash and putting it into their bags.

"Why don't you three come with me?" Kasey gestured at Maritza, Makena, and me to follow him, and he led us down to the water's edge, where several volunteers were setting up canoes.

"We get to use a canoe?" Makena said. "Cool!" We slapped our hands together in a three-way high five.

Kasey handed us life jackets. We put them on and climbed into a canoe, laughing and squealing. Kasey and Maritza each took an oar and paddled the canoe over to a fallen tree with plastic bags, bottles, cans, cups, and chunks of Styrofoam caught in its branches. Kasey handed us long

grabbers, and we fished all the stuff out of the water and put it in our garbage bags. I tried to keep an eye on the shore for Gran E, but picking up trash took all my focus.

"How did all this litter get here?" Maritza asked Kasey. "Did people just dump it?"

"Some of it," he replied. "Littering is illegal, but people sometimes dump garbage in out-of-the-way places where no one will see them do it. Like here."

"Why don't they just haul their garbage to the dump?" I asked.

"Because getting rid of garbage isn't free." He gestured to a pile of tires one of the work crews had collected. "Like these tires here—you have to pay a fee to take them to a tire shredder for recycling. You also have to pay to leave garbage at the dump. Some businesses avoid those fees by dumping their garbage into the river instead. If they're caught, they can be arrested and fined."

"Does this happen everywhere in DC?" Makena asked. "Or just here in Anacostia?"

"It happens all over," Kasey said, "but it's worse here on the east side of the river. This side is mostly Black folks, so the environment doesn't get monitored as closely. Factories are more likely to get away with polluting, and illegal dumping is more likely to be ignored."

"That's treating people on the east side like second-class

citizens," said Makena, her eyes flashing.

"Sounds like racism," I said.

Kasey nodded. "It's environmental injustice on top of racism. Unfortunately, it's how things have been for a long time. But we're fighting back, and we're making progress. The law is on our side."

"Is that law the Clean Water Act?" I asked. In fifth grade on Earth Day, we had learned about the Clean Air Act and the Clean Water Act.

"Yes, that's one of the laws we can use to enforce environmental regulations," Kasey explained. "But not everything you see here was deliberately dumped. In fact, a lot of things, like these plastic bags and bottles, just get blown into the water by accident or washed in from sewers during a storm. If you throw litter on the sidewalk, it can end up in the river."

"We read about that in school!" I exclaimed. "Pollution can even start out in another state. If the tide in the Chesapeake Bay gives it a push, stuff can float up the river for miles."

Kasey nodded. "The river connects many places."

"It connects people, too," I said, waving at Gia and Ashlyn, who were squealing and laughing as they helped drag an old chair out of the mud.

Finally, we paddled back to shore, our canoe loaded with

a full cargo of stuffed garbage bags. Kasey and I carried them up the path to the street, where everything would be collected by garbage trucks on Monday.

Ashlyn, Ziggy, and Gia were getting picked up at noon. I hurried over to say good-bye. "Thanks for coming, guys," I told them. Ashlyn gave me a hug.

"Anytime," said Ziggy.

"It was fun," said Gia.

I waved and quickly found Maritza and Makena. I'd invited them to meet my family and have lunch with us.

Bud, Dad, and my grandparents were sitting at the old picnic table. I introduced Makena and Itza, and we sat down to eat. Grandma Peeters had brought sandwiches for us.

I looked around. "Has anyone seen Gran E?"

"Nope," said Bud with his mouth full.

I checked my phone. Gran had texted me—she wouldn't be able to join us. She didn't say why. I felt a pang. Gran had said that wild horses wouldn't keep her away, yet she wasn't here. Grandma Peeters had promised me that she'd speak to Gran E when she saw her. Now that wouldn't happen.

THE RIVER AND ME

My grandparents left after lunch, and the rest of us got back to work. Bud and I helped Makena and Maritza comb through the ferns and shrubs, looking for smaller pieces of litter. Dad, Kasey, and his crew wrestled the lawn mower and an old sofa out of the river and dragged them up to the parking area so they could be hauled away. Then we all made a human chain and helped roll the tires through the woods and out to the parking area to be picked up for recycling. Kasey explained that tires are especially bad for the river, because as they deteriorate, they leach toxic chemicals and heavy metals into the water, hurting the fish and water plants.

By late afternoon, we had collected more than eighty bags of trash and recyclables and almost fifty tires!

I looked around. The grass was trampled, but seeing the

riverbank free of litter lifted my heart. I was just sorry that Gran E wasn't there to see it, too.

"Your other grandmother never showed, did she?" said Maritza, reading my mind.

I shook my head. "Guess I need a plan B."

"You'll think of one," said Makena. "Hey, I'll be at the food pantry tomorrow afternoon, if you want to come by."

"Sure! Thanks so much for coming, both of you," I said.

"It was fun," said Maritza. "Look what we accomplished."

Makena nodded. "The river looks so much better," she exclaimed. "It's so peaceful and pretty here now."

They were right. With a day of hard but fun work, we had healed part of the river. If only it could be this easy for my grandmothers to heal the rift between them.

A WORLD BY US

Chapter 10

The next morning, Dad drove me over to Riverfront Community Center and dropped me off there for a few hours. I found Makena talking to some people by the food pantry. She grinned and waved at me. Together, we headed down the hall toward the lounge.

"*Hola, amigas!*" Maritza called from the lobby.

"Maritza!" we cried happily. "You're here, too!"

"I asked my mom to drive me over after church." She caught up with us and pointed at the graphic on Makena's top. "Pretty! You must love butterflies."

"Did you guys know monarch butterflies are endangered?" I asked. "Seriously, we need to start taking better care of nature."

"Well, we made a good start on that yesterday," Makena pointed out.

"True. Still, I wish there was more we could do," I said. "I mean, it's going to be our world someday."

"Well, we don't need to wait until we grow up to make a difference," said Maritza. "Why don't we start *now*, making the kind of world *we* want to live in?"

We all sat down at the craft table. "I want to live in a world where the color of your skin doesn't matter," said Makena.

"Where a community can have people with different backgrounds and beliefs, but still be united," said Maritza.

"With liberty, equality, and justice for *all*," Makena added.

"With no racism and no pollution," I said, picking up a purple marker. On a piece of poster paper, I wrote the words *racism* and *pollution*, made circles around them, and then drew a slash through each circle.

Maritza grinned and picked up a red marker. She drew an octagon with the word *STOP*, like a stop sign, and underneath it, she wrote *racism*.

"That's what we're against—but what are we *for*?" asked Makena.

"*La comunidad*—community," Maritza suggested.

I picked up a blue marker and wrote *community*. I noticed it had the word *unity* in it, which seemed fitting.

"I think we've already started our first project, with the river cleanup," Makena pointed out.

"So, what's next?" asked Maritza.

"We could share online," I said, turning to Makena. "Like you do with your fashion posts, except we'll share what we're doing about pollution, and racism, and other things we care about."

"Other kids could share their stories, too," said Maritza. "Makena, can you show us how to start a website?"

Makena's eyes lit up. "Sure, if my parents say it's okay. I bet our ideas will go viral—and if enough kids join us, we'll be unstoppable!" She tilted her head, thinking. "What should we call it?"

"A world—by us," I announced, writing it out on a piece of poster board. I looked up at my friends. Somehow when I was with them, anything seemed possible. "That's what we'll call it—and that's what we'll *make* it."

As I did my homework that night, I couldn't stop thinking about our conversation. If we were going to tackle big problems like racism, then I had to start with the issue in my own family.

Mom and Dad believed my grandmothers would never get along. And it was clear that Gran E and Grandma Peeters would never come together on their own. But I wouldn't give up on them. They were my family; I had to try again. And I had to do it in a way that my grandmothers couldn't avoid each other. I chewed my pencil, thinking.

Tomorrow Bud had softball practice, so it would be just me and Gran E after school. That gave me an idea. I picked up my phone and texted Gran E.

> Let's go back to the swimming hole tomorrow. I have 2 surprises for you.

Then I called Grandma Peeters to make a plan.

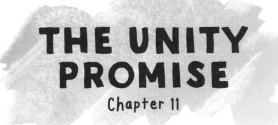

THE UNITY PROMISE

Chapter 11

On Monday, getting dressed for school, I put on the umoja locket from Gran E as well as the heart locket from Grandma Peeters. I had felt a sense of unity at the river cleanup; I wanted unity in my family, too.

At school, Ashlyn, Ziggy, Gia, and I looked for each other at lunch. We sat together in the cafeteria, sharing photos and stories from the river cleanup. We even had a competition over who had found the most disgusting garbage.

"I helped drag this ratty old armchair out of the mud," Gia bragged. "When I picked up the seat cushion, there were all these slugs and grubs and slimy things squirming around!"

"Yuck! Too bad my brother Bud wasn't on your work crew," I laughed. "He loves worms and gross stuff like that—the slimier, the better."

"Check *this*," said Ashlyn. "Behind a bush I found a soggy pizza box with half a pizza still inside it. It was totally green with mold, and it stunk so bad I almost threw up!"

"*Eewww!*" We all squealed and giggled.

"I can top that," Ziggy boasted. "I picked up a bag, and a

dead possum fell out! It was half skeleton, half sludge—and one eyeball was hanging by a thread!"

"You win, Ziggy!" I declared, as Ashlyn shrieked with delighted disgust.

Gia rolled her eyes. "He's making that up!"

"Seriously, I'm not!" Ziggy said, and we all laughed. Why had I ever thought we couldn't be friends?

"Thanks again for your hard work," I said. "I can't wait until my grandmother sees how beautiful her river is now."

After school, Gran E picked me up. "I see you're wearing the umoja necklace I gave you," she said as I slid into the front seat beside her.

I nodded. "It stands for unity, right?"

Gran nodded as she steered onto the road. "We could use more unity in this world, that's for sure."

"We could use more unity in our family, too," I said without missing a beat.

Her eyebrows went up. "Oh? And what do you mean by that? Something I should know about?"

"You do know about it," I replied. "I'm talking about you and Grandma Peeters."

Gran E pursed her lips. "What do *you* know about that?"

It was time to put it out there. "I know what happened when Mom and Dad got married. Grandma told me," I said. "She told me she feels awful for what she said about your neighborhood and for making my parents have the wedding reception at her house, when you wanted to have it at yours."

Gran looked a little shocked. She wasn't expecting this, that's for sure. I pressed on. "Grandma's a good person who said some wrong, racist things. But people can change." I took a deep breath and asked the crucial question. "If she apologized, would you give her another chance?"

Gran E kept her eyes on the road and continued driving, almost as if she hadn't heard me. When we arrived at the dead end, she parked and switched off the motor. Then she turned to me. "Evie, the truth is, when your grandmother said those hurtful things, she was judging me and my whole neighborhood, my community. Judging us by the color of our skin. And you know what? That made me afraid she would judge your mother the same way, and I couldn't bear to see that happen. So I never wanted anything to do with her. I know she's been a good grandmother to you and Bud, and I'm grateful for that, but—well, I just don't know."

I swallowed. I'd hoped that I could make things better between them, but it didn't sound promising. I was nervous about my plan, which involved an element of surprise. As we got out of the car, I said quickly, "I know that's why you didn't come to the river cleanup—because you didn't want to see Grandma Peeters. But if you should happen to see her one of these days—I mean, it could be sooner than you think—I hope you'll at least listen to what she has to say."

Gran E peered at me suspiciously. "Evette, are you trying to tell me something?"

I thought again about Ashlyn, Gia, Ziggy, and what I had thought of them on the first day of school. I had almost dropped my friendship with Ashlyn because of it. Yet they had pitched in at the river cleanup, and now we were all friends. None of that would have happened if I had stubbornly held on to my original thoughts about them— thoughts that turned out to be wrong.

I looked at Gran E. "Yes, I guess I am," I replied. "What I'm trying to tell you is not to judge a whole person for one thing they did or said. People can change and learn from their mistakes. Give Grandma Peeters a chance to show you how she can be better than she acted all those years ago."

We turned down the gravel path through the woods. In the late afternoon sun, the river's glassy surface reflected the tall trees like a mirror. The ferns and grasses were still trampled from all the activity on Saturday, but there wasn't a speck of litter to be seen.

"Oh my, isn't it pretty here now," Gran murmured. "It's just as I remember."

"Let's walk down to the water,"
I said, leading the way.

Beneath a spreading tree near the
riverbank, a woman in a big straw
hat was opening a picnic basket. She
looked up at us and waved.

Gran E recognized Grandma
Peeters and stopped in her tracks. "Was
this your plan all along?" she said under her breath.

I caught her hand. "Just give her a chance. Do it for me
and Bud." She pursed her lips, as if considering.

I held up my umoja necklace. "Do it for family unity.
I know you believe in unity, since you gave me this necklace. Please?"

Gran shook her head and muttered, "I just don't know
about this," but she let me lead her to the picnic table.

Grandma Peeters was setting out plates and a tall
thermos. She looked up with an anxious smile. "Thank you
for coming, Evon. It's been years since we've seen each other."

"Yes, Kathryn," said Gran E, "it has."

"It's good of you to come today," Grandma Peeters
plowed ahead. "I realize it's more than I deserve."

I kept my mouth shut. I was on pins and needles watching the two of them, wondering what would happen next.

Grandma Peeters cleared her throat and lifted a

bundle of sandwiches out of
the picnic basket. "What'll it be,
Evon—tuna on wheat or ham on rye?"

"Tuna's fine for me," said Gran E politely.

I let out a sigh of relief. So far, so good!

"I'll take ham," I said, passing out napkins and cups.

As we sat down and began eating, Grandma Peeters
spoke softly. "I have waited far too long to apologize to you,
Evon. But, well, better late than never, as they say. Evette
helped me to see that. So that's what I'm here to do today—
apologize for the wrong I did you."

Grandma paused and looked down at her napkin,
smoothing the creases. When she spoke again, her voice was
barely more than a whisper. "Just before our children got
married, I did something terribly insensitive and thought-
less. I didn't take time to gather the facts—I just went with
what I'd heard. I see now
how wrong and hurtful
that was. I didn't mean it
to be, but it was." She
twisted the napkin, then
smoothed it out again. "I'm
here to tell you how sorry
I am. It was a truly
awful thing to do,

I know that now, and I can honestly say I've regretted it ever since. I'm here to apologize from the bottom of my heart, and to make amends if I can."

Gran E stared out at the river for a long minute. Then she spoke. "Nia is my daughter and my only child. It felt as if you and your husband didn't think that the home where Nia was raised was good enough for your people. Then it occurred to me that you might think that my Nia was not good enough for your son Jason. I can't tell you how much that hurt."

Grandma Peeters bowed her head. "It was unforgivable. It was—racist. I know that now, and I know I don't have any right to expect forgiveness. But I do want you to know that I'm truly, truly sorry. If I could take it back, I would, in a heartbeat."

There was another long silence. Gran E took a sip of iced tea. At last she said, "Nothing can be accomplished by holding on to hurt feelings. I think mine are past their expiration date." Her chest rose in a big sigh, and her shoulders settled as though releasing a burden. "What hope is there for the rest of the world if two old ladies can't get past a problem in our own family?"

I looked back and forth from one grandmother to the other. "Well, we *are* one family," I said. "So we should all act like it, right?"

"I would like that," said Grandma Peeters, with a hopeful look at Gran E. "I want to set a better example of family togetherness for our grandchildren—if you'll give me that chance."

"I guess I'm willing if you are," Gran E said. "Now, are those deviled eggs I see?"

"What would a picnic be without them?" Grandma said, passing the platter with a smile—not the tight, nervous smile she had earlier, but a real one that lit up her blue eyes. "I baked a coconut cake, too. I didn't dare try a red velvet— I hear that's your specialty."

Under the table, I grabbed Gran E's hand and gave it a squeeze. My heart was too full to speak.

"This is a lovely spot," said Grandma Peeters. "Evette tells me you used to swim here as a girl."

"That I did. I hear you and your husband helped to clean it up," said Gran E. "I surely appreciate that."

"It was all Evette's idea. She got us involved in the river cleanup. She's a remarkable young lady, just like her mother." Grandma Peeters cut three slices of cake and passed them around. "Evette tells me you like knitting. So do I."

"Oh, yes, I've been knitting since I was a small girl," said Gran E.

"Hey, there's a cool knitting exhibit at Riverfront," I chimed in. "You'd both love it. Could we go there after this, so I can show it to you? It's not far from here."

"That does sound like fun," said Grandma Peeters.

"Sure, why not," said Gran E. "And this cake is delicious. I'd love the recipe."

Grandma Peeters smiled again. "It's an old family favorite. I'd be delighted to share it."

After we were done eating, Grandma Peeters and Gran E lingered at the picnic table, talking, so I got up to explore the woods. Sunlight filtered through the branches, making lacy shadows on the path. Suddenly, above the birdsong, I heard the loud rumble of a truck. Through the trees, a pickup sputtered as it slowly backed down the gravel access path that led from the street to the river. As I stopped to watch, the engine shut off, and a man jumped out. He looked vaguely familiar. I realized where I'd seen him—at the garage with Dad. What was Stan doing here?

I hid behind a bush and watched as he opened the

back gate of his truck and began throwing a bunch of old tires onto the ground.

"Hey!" I yelled, stepping out from behind the bush. "You can't do that! Those tires will pollute the river—and we just cleaned it up!"

Stan whipped around. His eyes widened when he saw me. "Don't report me, kid," he said. Before I could answer, he jumped into his truck and peeled away, leaving the tires.

"Evette, what's happening?" called Gran E.

"We heard shouting," called Grandma Peeters. "Are you okay?"

I turned. My grandmothers were coming up the path. "I'm fine—but I'm mad!" I told them what I'd seen.

"That man has some nerve, messing up our river!" said Gran E.

"Too bad we don't know who he is. He'd have to pay a hefty fine for littering by the river," said Grandma.

I caught my breath. I *did* know who the man was. Stan had helped out my dad when he had a flat, and his business was struggling. Still, that didn't make it okay to pollute.

I frowned at the pile of tires. One had rolled over a fern, which was standing up through the center of the tire like a potted plant. And that gave me an idea.

At dinner that night, I told Mom and Dad what I'd seen Stan do. "I don't want to get him in trouble—but I don't want him to get away with dumping his tires in the river, either."

"It's irresponsible," Bud declared. "Right, Mom? You always tell us we need to take responsibility for our stuff." Bud's stuff was usually strewn around the house, so he got this lecture often.

"Stan should certainly dispose of his tires in a responsible manner," Mom agreed.

I turned to Dad. "Could you call Stan and ask him to go get the tires he dumped and bring them to Riverfront?" I asked. "I have an idea for how to reuse them, but I'll need some help. Can you also cut me some pieces of plywood?"

Dad buttered a roll. "Evie, I'm happy to provide plywood, but I think you should call Stan yourself. Just tell him what you want him to do. I'm sure he'll be glad to help."

"He's in no position to refuse," Mom pointed out.

"Just tell him if he doesn't do what you say, he'll have to pay a big fat fine," Bud urged. My brother had a strong sense of justice. Mom and Dad were convinced that if he didn't become a farmer when he grew up, he'd be a judge.

"Thanks, Bud, I've got this," I told him.

It was time for World by Us, step two.

STEP TWO: PAINT AND MARIGOLDS
Chapter 12

Meet me at RCC Friday pm
wear old clothes
bring paint

Riverfront Community Center was having a festival to raise money for the food pantry, and I'd thought of a way to contribute. Friday after school, I met Makena and Maritza in the service area behind the building, where I'd asked Stan to deliver the tires. First, we hosed them off, and while they dried in the sun, I explained my idea for turning them into planters. Dad had cut me twelve squares of plywood, which we fitted into the bottom of each tire and glued in place. Now each tire could hold a large pot.

Then we broke out our paints. I painted one tire blue with colorful fish swimming around the rim, and wrote "Find UNITY in CommUNITY" in curly letters around another. Makena covered one with butterflies, and Maritza made geometric patterns. Then we painted several tires to look like gigantic doughnuts with icing and sprinkles on them. I wrote "ReTIRED from driving" on one tire and "Off-Road Use Only!" on another. Finally, we went wild spatter-painting the last few tires—and our clothes.

The day before, I'd found some old plastic pots stacked in Gran E's garage and asked if I could have them. "That's why I save stuff," she said. "You never know when you might have a use for it." Gran E had grown marigolds in her garden to keep beetles away from her cucumbers, but the cucumbers were done for the season, so she'd let me dig up the marigolds and plant them in the pots for my tire project.

"They look so pretty," Maritza exclaimed as we set the pots of marigolds inside the tires.

"Say cheese!" As Maritza and I struck silly poses, Makena shot photos to post on our World by Us site.

STEP TWO: PAINT AND MARIGOLDS

Saturday dawned sunny and warm—perfect for the festival. My family arrived early, and soon Makena and Maritza came and helped me set up our tire planters on the lawn as people began strolling in. There was live music on a small stage, Makena's uncle was there with his food truck, and people of all ages browsed the craft tables.

"What a creative way to use old tires," said a familiar voice. "How much are they?" I looked up, and Kasey grinned at me.

"Hi, Kasey!" I said. "We made them ourselves, from tires that were dumped at the river. They're twenty-five dollars each, but you can have a discount."

He laughed. "I don't mind paying full price. It's for a good cause."

The tires sold quickly, and soon we only had two left.

"Hey, are these my old tires? They look pretty nice!" It was Stan. I had invited him when I called him to ask for the tires. "I want you to know, I won't dump tires again," he said.

"Glad to hear it," I replied. "Tires should be recycled. If you don't want to pay to shred them, then why don't you sell these planters at your shop? We could make more for you."

"Well now, that's an idea!" Stan said. "You're giving me

and my tires another chance." He pulled out his wallet. "I'll buy those last two planters from you. They'll look real nice at my garage, gussy the place up a bit. If customers want more, I'll take you up on your offer, and split the profits with the community center here. How does that sound?"

I grinned. Everyone deserved another chance—even old tires! "It's a deal," I told Stan, and we shook on it.

I turned to Makena and Maritza. "We're all sold out. Let's go get some eats!"

We bought grilled cheese sandwiches from Makena's uncle's food truck and took them across the lawn to eat on the benches at the river's edge. The shimmering water looked inviting, even though I knew that it still was too polluted to swim in. But there are laws in place to clean it up. It will take time, but we're making progress. At Gran E's swimming spot, we had made a difference. And if enough people care and pitch in, we can rescue all our rivers from pollution.

I know the world has many problems, just as there are many kinds of pollution in the river. But with the sunshine and the music and good friends beside me, I felt a wave of hope rise in my chest. As long as we can imagine a better world, we can make it happen. When people come together, we can do remarkable things. The river taught me that.

Meet the Author
SHARON DENNIS WYETH

Sharon, age 5

When I was a girl, people often asked me what race I was. I'd say "I'm Negro" or "I'm Black," but they didn't believe me. I learned that it's impossible to know who someone really is from their appearance. Seeing my light skin, no one guessed that I was a Black kid. Yet I was classified as "Colored" on my birth certificate, the same as both my parents. I attended Black schools and churches. From my appearance, it was plain that some of my ancestors were White, yet these ancestors were never spoken of. My family's mixed-race heritage was a mystery I wanted to solve.

So I asked questions of my grandparents and did my own research. I learned that my African heritage originated in the Tikar, Fulani, and Hausa tribes of Cameroon. My Irish great-grandmother, Frances, came to the United States as an indentured servant and fell in love with a free man of color. A great-grandfather named George was born into slavery but freed at age three and inherited a fortune from the White father who owned him. George was the White man's only son, and George and his mother and sister were the man's only family.

More than a few times in my family, love crossed the color line.

My family lived in Anacostia, and like Evette I spent a lot of time with my grandparents. At Anacostia High School, a teacher once told me that I couldn't run for president of the student council because I was "Negro." When I told my mother, she visited the principal. I did run for student council, ending the practice of racial disqualification.

In first grade, I once got lost walking home. A lady found me and took me to her house. I'd memorized my phone number, so she called my mother and took me home. But what stands out in my mind is what the lady said to a friend who was in her apartment: "Look what I found, a little White child. She's lost, and I'm going to take her home."

Well, I had no idea what she meant! My parents hadn't told me about Black and White. I didn't know that everyone had a box they belonged in and according to my birth certificate I belonged in the Black box. The lady who found me had no way of knowing that either, because I had light skin. To her I was "a little White child." I wouldn't have known what to call her, because I didn't know about the White and Black boxes yet. I do remember what she looked like— she was tall, with dark hair and skin the same color as my mother's, which was brown. But the important thing about her was that she was going to take me home! Race didn't matter.

Sharon, age 9

REAL KIDS, REAL CHANGE

Jocelyn C., Danny C., and Sofia R. helped their school cafeteria switch to reusable spoons and forks.

When eleven-year-old Jocelyn learned that her cafeteria was throwing away 1,000 plastic spoons and forks every day, she talked to the principal to try to change things. The principal had a proposition for her: If Jocelyn and her fifth-grade class could teach other students about reducing waste and convince them to keep reusable utensils out of the trash, the school would make the switch.

Danny and Sofia joined the effort, and the three classmates started creating posters and lesson plans about reducing plastic waste. Then they taught their lessons to every class in the school, in both English and Spanish! They adjusted their message to suit kids of different ages so that everyone could understand.

When the cafeteria switched to reusable utensils, every fifth-grader volunteered to monitor the garbage cans and remind students to put spoons and forks in the right places. The new program worked great!

READER QUESTIONS

Use these questions to spark conversations about Evette's story.

1. When Ziggy asks Evette "Are you Black or White?" why does this question bother her?

2. When Evette first sees Ashlyn's new hairstyle and the way Ashlyn's friends Gia and Ziggy are dressed, how does she react? How does Evette's attitude change?

3. How does Evette's change of attitude toward Ashlyn, Gia, and Ziggy help her decide what to do about the rift between her grandmothers?

4. Evette organizes a river cleanup. What other things does she do in her story to protect the environment?

5. At the end of her story, Evette says, "I felt a wave of hope rise in my chest." Why?

6. What things does Evette learn in her story? How does she learn them?

YOUR LIFESTYLE CAN HELP THE EARTH. HERE'S HOW:

Shop Smart: Buy used clothes, books, and games instead of new ones—or have a clothing swap with your friends! Buy things that will last a long time. Avoid packaging, which usually turns into trash. Especially avoid plastic! It lasts almost forever.

Fashion Challenge: Visit a thrift or secondhand shop with a friend or two. Each of you creates an outfit using only clothes and accessories you find there. When you get home, put on a fashion show with your new-old clothes!

Creative Party: Instead of buying single-use party decorations, make your own. Raid your basement and recycling bins, and see what kind of decor you can create. Gifts can be wrapped in old calendar pages or colorful magazine pages. Serve food using your regular dishes and silverware.

Is your community facing drought? Wildfire? Pollution? Learn about local environmental issues by reading articles on the internet or in the newspaper. Then do a school report so more people know about the problem and what can be done to fix it. Just by spreading the news, you're helping.

For more tips on taking good care of the planet, read *Love the Earth*

YOU CAN HELP END RACISM. HERE'S HOW TO GET STARTED:

Watch movies and documentaries about people in the US or other countries whose lives are unlike yours. How are these people different from stereotypes you have heard?

Get to know people of different races and backgrounds. Be friendly and patient; bonds can take a while to form. (If they don't, that's okay; nobody clicks with everyone.) Do fun activities that you both enjoy. Most of all, be real. True friendship is built on being yourself and sharing the real you with another person.

Treat others with empathy and compassion, even when you disagree. Be a good listener, and try to see the world through their eyes. Be kind, and don't judge. Keep your heart and mind open to different experiences and opinions.

If you learn some tough truths that make you feel upset, angry, or guilty, find support by talking to a trusted adult or older sibling. You're creating positive change in the world because you care. That's something to feel good about!

To learn more about fighting racism, read
A Smart Girl's Guide: Race & Inclusion

LOOK FOR BOOKS ABOUT
MAKENA AND MARITZA

Makena Williams has a passion for fashion. She loves putting clothes together in unexpected ways. When school went virtual because of the pandemic, Makena started sharing her style by posting her OOTD (outfit of the day). Now she's back to school in person and meeting some of her fashion followers for the first time. Clothes are a way for Makena to connect with others. But some people don't see Makena for who she is. They only see her as a Black girl, and they make unfair assumptions. After she experiences a racist incident in her own neighborhood, Makena decides to use fashion to speak up about injustice. Her style becomes her story.

Maritza Ochoa is Bolivian on her mother's side, Mexican on her father's side, and 100 percent American soccer player. She dreams of playing for the US women's soccer team, and even coaching it someday. Her soccer teammate Violeta shares those dreams, too, but for her they are harder to reach. Violeta's family immigrated to the United States from El Salvador, and now her uncle may be sent back there, far away from his US family. Without the money he earns and the love and support he provides, the family is in distress. Maritza believes that families belong together. Can she find a way to help Violeta's family? With her friends Evette and Makena cheering her on, Maritza finds the courage to lead with her heart.

*Each sold separately. Find more books online at **americangirl.com**.*